THREE DAYS ON A RIVER
IN A RED CANOE

by Vera B. Williams

GREENWILLOW BOOKS • NEW YORK

*Thanks for rivers
and friends,
big and small*

Greenwillow Books,
a division of
William Morrow & Company, Inc.,
1350 Avenue of the Americas,
New York, NY 10019.
Printed in the
United States of America

15 14 13 12 11 10 9 8 7

Library of Congress
Cataloging in Publication Data
Williams, Vera B
Three days on a river
in a red canoe.
Summary:
Mother, Aunt Rosie, and
two children make a three-day
camping trip by canoe.
[1. Canoes and canoeing
—Fiction. 2. Camping—
Fiction] I. Title.
PZ7.W6685Th   [E]   80-23893
ISBN 0-688-80307-5
ISBN 0-688-84307-7 (lib. bdg.)

I was the one who first noticed the red canoe for sale in a yard on the way home from school.

My mom and my aunt Rosie and my cousin Sam
and I put our money together and bought it.
The people who sold it to us threw in two
paddles and two big old life jackets.

As soon as we got home with the canoe, Aunt Rosie and Mom took out their maps. The canoe trips they had taken before Sam or I was even born were marked in colors. They found a three-day trip that could be just right for us. Then we made lists of what we needed.

Then we went shopping.

Here are Sam and I in the store in new life jackets.

They cost a lot, but Aunt Rosie and Mom agreed we had to have them. And an extra paddle. And twenty feet of new rope. We also bought some packages of freeze-dried chicken and some dried apricots.

Here is everything we need for the trip. The food is packed tight in waterproof sacks. My cat Sixtoes is sitting on a sleeping bag. I wanted to take him, but Mom says a canoe is no place for a cat. I promised Sixtoes to bring him back a fish. Next to my shoes and Sam's shoes are new pocketknives. We never even noticed Aunt Rosie buying them for us in the store today.

 WE DROVE AND DROVE  AND DROVE AND DROVE 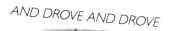 AND DROVE AND DROVE  AND DROVE AND DROVE  AND DROVE AND DROVE

Here we are on our way early in the morning.

 AND DROVE AND DROVE  AND DROVE AND DROVE  AND DROVE AND DROVE  AND DROVE AND DROVE  AND DROVE AND DROVE

WE DROVE AND DROVE

We drove all day. Now we are at the place Aunt Rosie and Mom had chosen for our first camp. We start on the river in the morning. Sam and I unloaded the car. Mom and Aunt Rosie put up the tent. We hurried to get inside before it got too dark and the mosquitoes took too many bites out of us. We lay in our tent listening to the river.

When I poked my head out in the morning,
everything was wet. Yet it wasn't even raining.
We couldn't see our car. We could hardly see the river.

We carried
our canoe
down to the
water anyway.

Here we are setting out for a small island it shows on the map.
We've packed all our things into the canoe. We are going
to fix our breakfast on the island when the sun
warms up the river and dries up the mist.

Here are Mom and Aunt Rosie paddling into a part of the river like a hot green tunnel. I fell asleep. I think Sam did too. It's good Mom and Rosie didn't. Right here is where they heard the roaring of the waterfall. But they had been listening for it. It was marked on their maps.

Here I am looking over the edge.

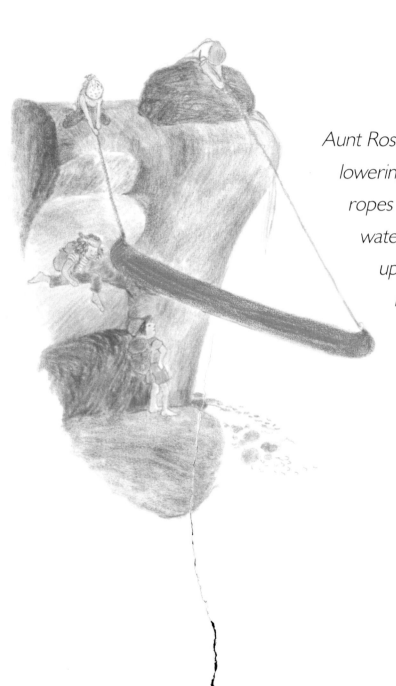

Aunt Rosie and Mom are
lowering the canoe by
ropes down over the
waterfall. Sam and I climb
up and down until we
have carried all the gear
to the bottom. We are
going to camp here even
though it's still early.

Here's our shower.

This is our kitchen. Aunt Rosie is the cook tonight.
We are going to try the crayfish we caught along
with our chicken and rice. For dessert Aunt Rosie
showed us how to cook fruit stew and dumplings.

This is the sink. You can stand right in it.
The rocks make all the shelves
and drainboards you need.
We use the sand as scouring powder.

Mom shows us some knots
we can use to tie up the canoe
and in putting up the tent.

TWO HALF HITCHES

1

PASS THE ROPE AROUND
A TREE OR STUMP

2

WITH YOUR LEFT HAND,
HOLD THE ROPE AT THE POINT
WHERE IT CROSSES OVER THE
LONGER PART OF THE ROPE

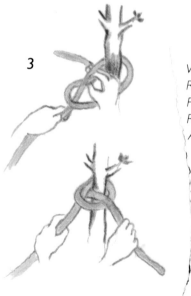

3

WITH YOUR RIGHT HAND,
REACH THROUGH THE LOOP
FOR THE SHORT END OF THE
ROPE. PULL THE END THROUGH
AND TIGHTEN THE LOOP

REPEAT 2 AND 3

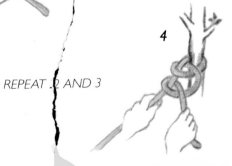

4

FIRE

You don't need a bonfire to cook on.
Aunt Rosie made this kind of fire.
She kept it hot by adding small sticks.

DUMPLINGS

I CUP DUMPLING-PANCAKE MIX (PAGE 6)
½ CUP OF WATER

Make a well in the mix. Pour in most of the water. Mix quickly. Use only enough water to make a dough as thick as soft ice cream.
Lumps don't matter. Push little spoonfuls of dumpling onto the simmering fruit as fast as you can. Cover. Cook until the dumplings are just done but not hard —about 10 minutes.

FRUIT STEW

3 HANDFULS OF DRIED APRICOTS (OR PEACHES)
HONEY OR SUGAR TO TASTE
ABOUT 3 CUPS OF WATER

Add enough water to the plastic bag to cover the fruit. Do this when you first make camp.

When you are ready to cook, put the fruit, all the water, and the sweetening in a pot.
Cover, and boil slowly.
Stir often.

Don't let the apricots burn. If water cooks away, add more. This fruit stew should be juicy. Cook till apricots are soft— about half an hour.

P.S. Don't burn your tongues.
We burned ours.

SAM AND I PUT UP
THE TENT BY OURSELVES

AUNT ROSIE TOLD ME
TO USE THE BACK
OF THE AXHEAD

SAM USED A ROCK

IT'S HARD TO GET THE PEGS IN
TIGHT SO THEY DON'T PULL OUT

YOU HAVE TO PULL
THE CORDS TIGHT TOO
SO THE TENT WON'T BE
LIKE AN OLD BALLOON

AND YOU HAVE TO TIE
A KIND OF KNOT
YOU CAN UNTIE EASILY

THIS IS AN EXTRA ROOF
CALLED A FLY

THE TENT CLOTH HAS TO LET IN AIR,
SO BY ITSELF IT CAN'T BE WATERPROOF

After supper we build up our fire and sit beside it. Mom tells
us stories about the animals that like the nighttime. We watched
the stars and the sparks of our fire going up to join them.

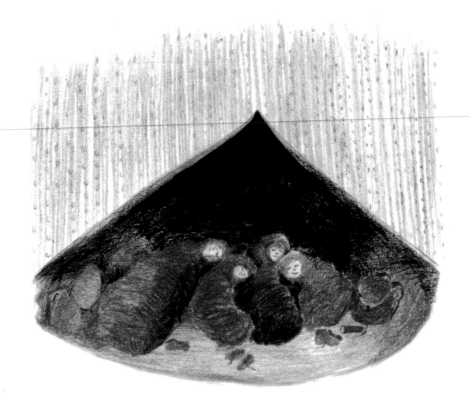

Sam isn't much of a weather predictor. But the rain didn't bother us. We put up the tent so well hardly a drop of water came through. In the morning we sat up in our sleeping bags and ate crackers and raisins. Aunt Rosie made cocoa on the little camping stove.

We set out on the river with all our
things even though it was pouring rain.
I am shaking my paddle at the sky
and yelling.

Suddenly as we came around this bend
in the river the sun came out through
a hole in the clouds. A big rainbow
spread across the sky.

SPOTTED SUNFISH   BULLHEAD CATFISH   REDFIN PICKEREL   YELLOW PERCH

SCALE CARP   BROOK TROUT   BLACK CRAPPIE   COMMON WHITE SUCKER

The rainbow faded away and fish started to jump all around us.
We got the fishing lines baited and into the water. Sam caught the
first fish. Then I caught one. Then Aunt Rosie caught two in a row.
Afterward we spread out our things to dry on a sandy beach.

What Mom and Aunt Rosie like to do best is take the canoe through fast-moving water. They can follow all the curves of the current.
In the afternoon we canoe without stopping. Sam and I paddle too.

We came to a place where the river spread
out through a meadow. Grass grows right out of
the water and we canoed in the grass. It came up over
our heads and hid us. Aunt Rosie put her hand over my
mouth so I wouldn't frighten away the moose and her calf. But even
so, when they got wind of us, they ran right back into the woods.

When we discovered this island, we all agreed it was the place to
spend our third night. We plan to sleep right out under those trees.
The tent is up just in case of rain. The big dipper is out. The Milky
Way is spread right across the sky. There isn't one mosquito because
of the breeze.

That breeze turned into a wild wind in the middle of the night. Mom says it was almost hurricane strength. We caught the tent and the canoe just before the wind carried them off down the river. We did lose one pot and one cup. We spent the rest of the night curled up in the bushes. The branches creaked and whooshed all night long.

GREAT BLUE HERON

In the morning we can't believe this is the same river. It's so still.
Twigs and leaves and flowers float around us as we start our last
day on the river. We watch a muskrat swimming. A heron dives
for a fish. We feed crumbs to the ducks. Cows watch us having
a river visit.

WHISTLING   MALLARD   CANADA GOOSE
SWAN   DUCK

We canoe through a town. We come to a low stone bridge.
Sam gets excited. He stands up to wave. Mom yells,
"Sit down!" I reach over and pull him down.

Aunt Rosie and Mom brace hard on the other side. This keeps
our canoe and everything in it from turning over.

But Sam ends up in the water. He swims to the rope Aunt Rosie
throws out to him and we tow him to shore. Mom doesn't say
much, but she looks upset. Aunt Rosie looks scared.
Sam changes to dry clothes and we canoe on.

Just past the train bridge Aunt Rosie asks Sam to stand up and see
what's ahead. He gets up as though the canoe were a baby's cradle.
He reports that the river is ending in a big lake. He says it looks
like the edge of the world on the other side.

Aunt Rosie says that's because we're coming to the town dam.
Mom points the canoe to cross the lake. There's no current
and the wind is against us. I'm glad it's slow going.

When we get to the other side, our trip will be over.

And here we are … taking our canoe out onto the bank. Aunt Rosie showed me on the map where the river goes from here. She says it travels on through rocky places with lots of rapids. Someday, after lots of practice, we can go there.

But now we must catch a fish for my cat Sixtoes. And Aunt
Rosie is going to talk with other campers and find a lift back
to our car Ladybug so we can get home tonight. Mom says
canoeing back up the river against the current would be very,
very hard even if we had time.

Way past midnight we turn into our own street. One
by one we stumble into the house. I go to sleep to the
sound of Sixtoes chewing on his fish. It seems I can
still hear the sound of the river running over the rocks.